P9-CSC-162

Lauren Child

Slightly Invisible

Featuring Charlie and Lola

with a special appearance by Soren Lorensen

CP
Candlewick Press

For the original Marv
and his sister, Martha, and
his brother, Vincent,

and

for Conrad and his brother, Enzo

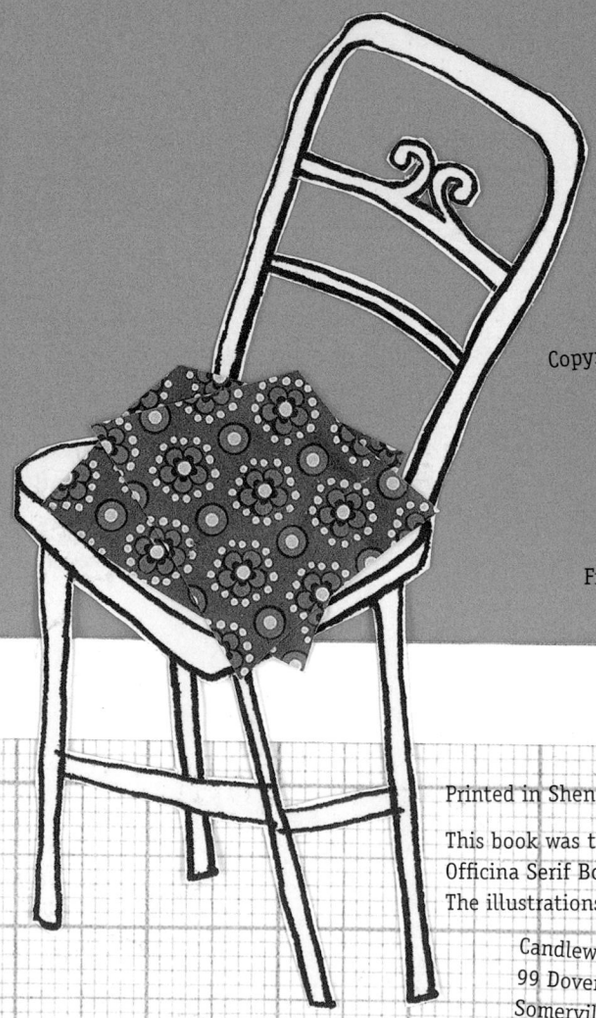

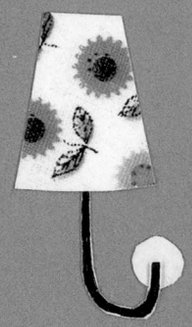

Copyright © 2010 by Lauren Child

All rights reserved. No part of this book may be reproduced, transmitted, or stored in an information retrieval system in any form or by any means, graphic, electronic, or mechanical, including photocopying, taping, and recording, without prior written permission from the publisher.

First U.S. edition 2011

First published in Great Britain in 2010 by Orchard Books, London

Library of Congress Cataloging-in-Publication Data is available.
Library of Congress Catalog Card Number pending
ISBN 978-0-7636-5347-7

11 12 13 14 15 16 WKT 10 9 8 7 6 5 4 3 2 1

Printed in Shenzhen, Guangdong, China

This book was typeset in
Officina Serif Book and Badloc.
The illustrations were done in mixed media.

Candlewick Press
99 Dover Street
Somerville, Massachusetts 02144

visit us at www.candlewick.com

I have this little sister, Lola.
She is small and very funny.
She always wants to know what I am up to, and
she always wants to do what I am doing.
She NEVER wants to be anywhere without me.

Most of the time this is fine.
But sometimes I just want to be by myself
ON MY OWN with just Marv.

Marv is my best friend, and usually we like
to spend our time looking for strange
and **tricky** creatures.

Lola does
not think
this is fun.

Last week Mary and I were busy floating in OUTER SPACE looking for
Martians.

and Lola stepped on our spaceship.
We had to walk back to Earth.

And one time,

when we had just discovered this amazing

SEA MONSTER at the bottom of the ocean,

Lola said she wanted to take it for a ride in her cart.

And yesterday,
just when
Marv and I
were
creeping up on the most STRANGE and

terrifyingly tricky creature
in the UNIVERSE,
Lola's rabbit
made a
squeaking
noise
and he ran off.

So this time I said,

"Today, Lola, just for once,
I want to play with Marv
by **myself** on
my own.

You see, we are inventing a
very **inventive** invention."

"What **is** it?" says Lola.

"What's it
top secret
for?"
says
Lola.

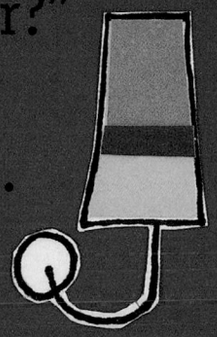

"It's a
potion for
helping
us catch
strange
and
tricky
creatures,"
says Marv.

"Oh," says Lola.
"How does it **do that**?"

"By turning you
invisible,"
Marv says.

"Oh,"
says Lola.

"Would
you
maybe
like to
have a
tea party
instead?"

"LOLA!" I say,
"Will you STOP bothering us
and interrupting!"
Lola says,
"I will NOT
do
bothering, and I will
NOT do interrupting.
You
won't even
know
I am here."

So
Marv and I
invent
an invisibility
potion.
It is
made
from pink
milk,
a tiny
drop of banana,
and a
secret
INVISIBLE
INGREDIENT
that no one
except us
can see.

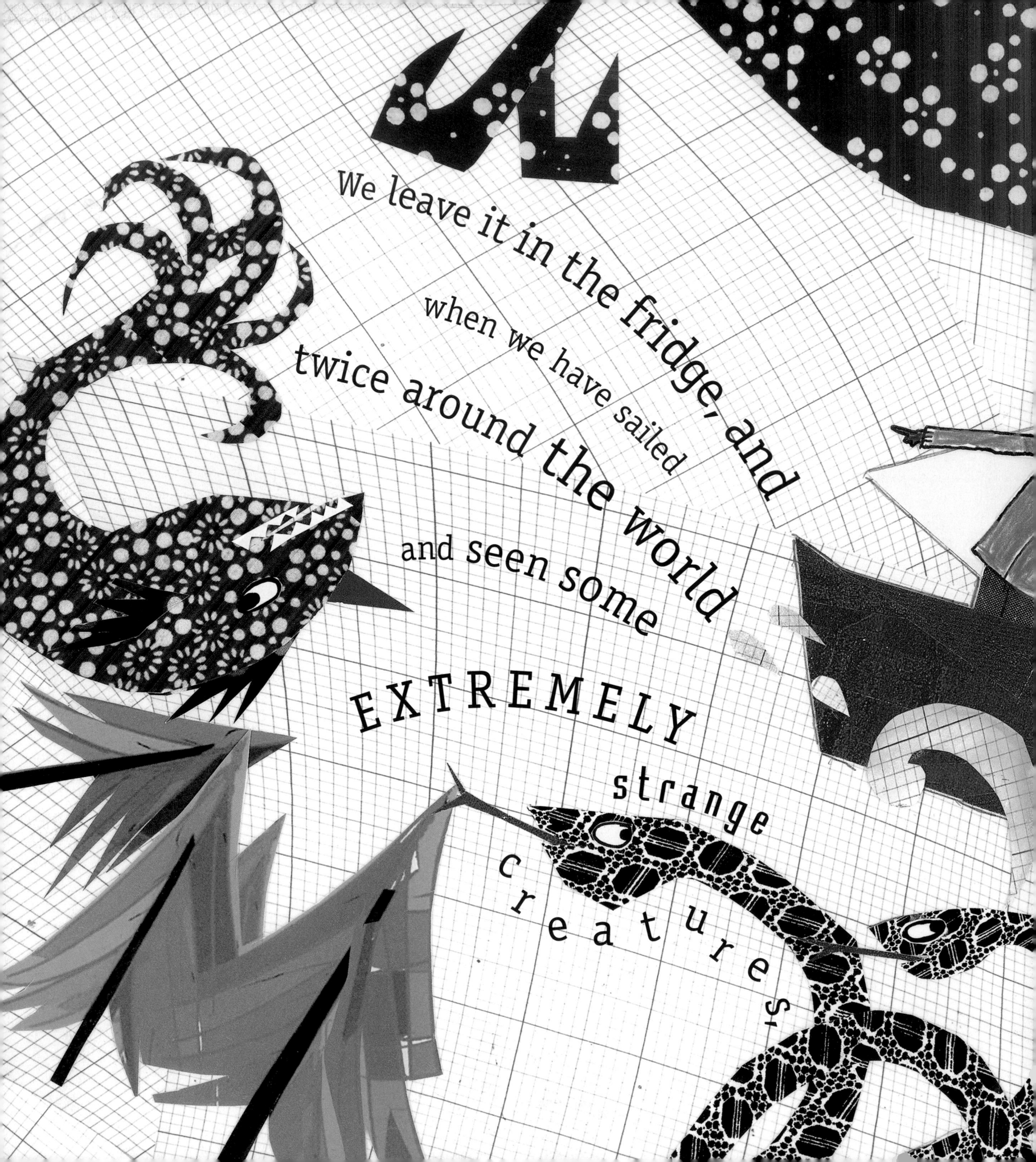
We leave it in the fridge, and
when we have sailed
twice around the world
and seen some
EXTREMELY
strange
creatures

but not **one** single **tricky** one,

we decide to

have a **snack.**

Sailing around
the world can
make you quite
peckish.

But when we go into the kitchen,
we get a bit of a fright

because there

is a

STRANGE and

terrifyingly **tricky**

creature,

looking very hungry

indeed.

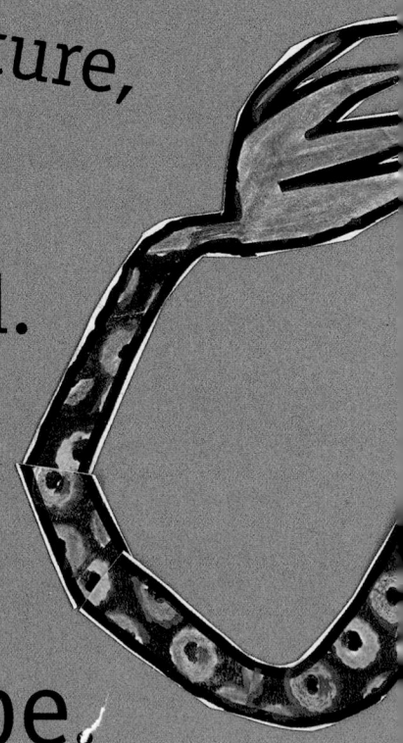

There is
no escape.

We quickly open the fridge door
but we find
to grab our invisibility potion,
that SOMEONE
Charlie
has already drunk it.

"Lola!" I shout. "What have you done with our potion?"
But Lola is nowhere to be seen.
We look everywhere.

But all we can hear is a tiny voice. . . .

It sounds as if it is coming from a long way away.

"Where are you?"

I shout.

"I am over here. You probably cannot see me because I am invisible."

But when I look under Mom and Dad's bed, there she is, talking away.

"Who are you talking to?" I say.

"My friend Soren Lorensen,"
says Lola.

I say, "LOLA, did you drink our
invisibility potion?"

Lola says,
"Oh, I only had a small sip.
Soren Lorensen had much more than
I did. That's why he is more
invisible than me."

I say, "You are NOT INVISIBLE,
not even one bit."

"How do you know?" says Lola.

"Because we can SEE you,
of course," says Marv.

And Lola says,
"You can only see me because
you know what I look like.
You can't see Soren Lorensen
at all."

"That's because there is NO such person as Soren Lorensen," I say.
"Well, if there is no such person,

then who ate all the cookies?" says Lola.
Marv says, "WHAT? Your friend Soren Lorensen ate all the cookies?"
Charlie
Lola says, "Oh, yes. I am afraid Soren Lorensen is quite greedy."

"Lola," I say, "now we will never catch the MOST STRANGE and terrifyingly **tricky** creature in the universe."

"Why not?" says Lola.

"Because we can't CREEP UP on him," says Marv.

"Don't worry," says Lola. "Soren Lorensen will **catch** him."

"Really?" I say.

"Oh, yes," says Lola.
"All you will need is
a tea set
and a little cart
and also a rabbit, of course."

"REALLY?" I say.

"Oh yes,
and you MUST
absolutely get one or
three glasses of
pink milk, too."

"WHAT?
All the
pink milk?"
says Marv.

"Yes,
completely,"
says Lola.

So we set off to find the
MOST STRANGE and terrifyingly tricky
creature in the universe.
I say, "What is the tea set for, Lola?"
And she says, "Tricky creatures love tea."
And
Marv
says,
"What is the
rabbit
for,
Lola?"

"For the pink milk, of course."
Lola says,
"But why do we need a little cart?"
I say,
of rabbits."
frightened
are creatures
Tricky you up.
And Mary says, "What is the pink milk for, Lola?"
gobbling
creature from the stop
"To
And Lola says,
And Lola says, "You will see."

Soon we find ourselves right in the middle of the deep, dark forest where the MOST STRANGE and terrifyingly **tricky** creature lives.

And Lola whispers,
"Shhh, Soren Lorensen is
talking, and he says we
must be very,
extremely
quiet.

Don't
make
even a
squeak."

"I can't hear him talking," says Marv.

"You can't **hear** him because he is INVISIBLE," says Lola.

"You CAN hear invisible people," I say.

Marv says, "There are no such things as **invisible** voices."

Lola says, "Not Soren Lorensen, because his **voice** is invisible **too**."

Lola says,
"If there are
no such things as
invisible voices,
then
why can't
you hear him?"

"SHHH," I whisper.
"Something is
coming."

AND THEN THERE HE IS,

the most **strange** and terrifyingly **tricky** creature in the universe,
about to gobble us up . . .

"Show him the rabbit!"

says Lola.

And just like that

we have

CAUGHT

HIM.

And there is
no escape for
the MOST STRANGE
and
terrifyingly tricky creature
in the
universe.

"See?" shouts Lola.
"I told you Soren Lorensen knew how to
catch the most strangest and
TRICKY creature."

"How did he do it?" I say.

"Well," says Lola,
"EVERYBODY loves tea parties."

"So who gets to drink the
pink milk?" says Marv.

"Oh, that is for
Soren Lorensen,"
says Lola.

"Catching strange
and tricky creatures
makes him quite
thirsty."

"Now,"
says Lola,

"it was fun
to play with
you and Marv,
but please
DON'T do any
bothering or
interrupting...."

"Soren Lorensen would like to
drink his pink milk all by himself,
with just me on his own."